Weekly Reader Children's Book Club presents

Mousekin's Close Call

Story and Pictures by EDNA MILLER

Prentice-Hall, Inc., Englewood Cliffs, N.J.

Printed in the United States of America

Prentice-Hall International, Inc., London
Prentice-Hall of Australia, Pty. Ltd., North Sydney
Prentice-Hall of Canada, Ltd., Toronto
Prentice-Hall of India Private Ltd., New Delhi
Prentice-Hall of Japan, Inc., Tokyo
Prentice-Hall of Southeast Asia Pte. Ltd., Singapore

10 9 8 7 6 5 4 3

Library of Congress Cataloging in Publication Data

Miller, Edna.
    Mousekin's close call.

    SUMMARY: Mousekin decides to try some defense
techniques to avoid becoming a victim of the bigger
forest animals.
    1. Mice—Legends and stories. [1. Mice—
Fiction.   2. Forest animals—Fiction.   3. Animal
defenses—Fiction]   I. Title.
PZ10.3.M5817Mm   [E]   77-27571
ISBN 0-13-604207-4
        0-13-604199-X (P.B.K.)

To The Children of
Vermont Achievement Center

Mousekin watched the trees grow dark.
He heard the night wind whisper.
It was time for the white-footed mouse to wake
and hunt for food in the forest.

Before Mousekin could finish cleaning his coat
and scamper outside his door,
he heard a snapping of branches; a crash of leaves.
It was a dreadful sound.

In the green dark shadows beneath him
Mousekin could see a fox circling and sniffing about.
Another creature, lying still, looked dead.
The fox barked once; then turned around,
and disappeared into the forest.
He would hunt a livelier dinner.

When Mousekin was certain the fox had gone
he hurried down the tree
to a pile of leaves where an oppossum lay,
motionless, on its side.

Its eyes were closed.
Its tongue hung limp
between half open jaws.
Mousekin didn't know the 'possum
just *pretended* to be dead.

As he stretched to sniff the fallen creature,
one bright eye opened wide.

And then. . . . HISSSSSSssssssssssssssss!

When Mousekin dared to look again,
the oppossum had climbed a tree.

Mousekin had seen this trick played before.
Often animals pretended to be wounded or dead.
They used this trick to fool other creatures
who might want them for their dinner.
They weren't as fast as a white-footed mouse.

A hog-nosed snake had pretended to be dead.

Then, like the 'possum, it had raced away
when danger passed.

Mousekin had seen a deer
pretending to be lame.
She limped along as though in pain.
Her one foot barely touching the ground

Hungry animals would chase *her*
instead of her little fawn.
When she had led the creatures far
and knew her fawn would be safe
she bounded away on all four legs.

By pretending her wing was broken,
a quail coaxed a bobcat to follow.

She led him away
from her chicks in the woods
and then flew up and away.

There was no need for Mousekin to pretend
if a fox or a bobcat chased him.
He was fast and he was small.
He could duck and hide in tiny places.
He could climb the highest tree.

His large bright eyes could see in darkness.
His silken ears could catch the smallest sound
as he hurried through the forest to a pond.

Mousekin gathered weed seeds
to build his winter store.
His adventure with the 'possum
had kept him from his work.
Night would soon be over
and a mouse must hide in the day.

Other creatures hunted then
but not for seeds and berries.

In the first pale light of day,
a swamp sparrow called to Mousekin,
warning him to hide.

But Mousekin was stuffing his cheeks with seeds.
He was much too busy to *listen*.

As Mousekin nibbled the fruit on the ground
a watching weasel sprang.
Mousekin had not been *looking*.

Razor sharp teeth held Mousekin.
The weasel had caught his prey.

The swamp sparrow called from the reeds again.
This time it was an angry warning.
The sparrow had spied the weasel coming
too close to her nest on the ground.
She flew at the intruder
in a sudden rush of wings.

The fury of the bird's attack confused the hungry weasel.
He couldn't fight back holding onto his dinner.

Dropping Mousekin, the weasel ran.

Mousekin lay still on a cover of leaves.
His eyes were closed. He scarcely breathed.
Mousekin was frozen with fear.
He was not pretending.

The sparrow stayed near eating seeds
that Mousekin had gathered for winter.
She was ready for flight, or ready to fight
if the weasel dare return.
The sparrow had learned about danger
from other creatures when she was young.
Now she had only one strong leg to use
when hopping near the pond.
She wasn't pretending either.

When Mousekin recovered from his fright
he stretched and cleaned his coat . . .
a much wiser mouse for his close call.
He would remember to stop, look and listen.

Mousekin would remember the sparrow
that hopped on one strong leg.
She had been *really* injured.
She was very brave.